SO-AJI-542

This edition ©Ward Lock Limited 1989

First published in the United States
in 1990 by Gallery Books,
an imprint of W.H. Smith Publishers, Inc.,
112 Madison Avenue, New York 10016.

Gallery Books are available for bulk purchase for sales
promotions and premium use. For details write or telephone
the Manager of Special Sales, W.H. Smith Publishers, Inc.,
112 Madison Avenue, New York, New York 10016. (212) 532-6600.

ISBN 0-8317-0974-X

All rights reserved. No part of this
publication may be reproduced, stored
in a retrieval system, or transmitted, in
any form or by any means electronic,
mechanical, photocopying, recording,
or otherwise, without the prior
permission of the Copyright owners.

Printed and bound in Hungary

THE BRAMBLEDOWN TALES

TINY CHICK'S TAIL

GALLERY BOOKS

An Imprint of W. H. Smith Publishers Inc

112 Madison Avenue

New York, New York 10016

One voice is louder than all the rest

Chapter One

A TAIL LIKE DADDY'S

In a fold in the hills is a little village called Brambledown. Do you know it? To the north is a dark, dense wood which keeps out the cold wind. To the south is a river silver with sunshine and fish. To the west is an orchard full of fruit trees, and to the east runs the road where the villagers come and go.

Listen! When the wind blows over the hills, you might hear the sounds of Brambledown – the people calling, "Hello! How are you?" – the cartwheels creaking, the bell ringing over the door of the village shop. And of course you will hear the oink-squeak-baa-quack of Brambledown Farm.

In the mornings, one voice is louder than all the rest.

"Cock-a-doodle-do!"

That's Mr Cock Chick the cockerel, crowing hello to the spring morning. He struts up and down the farmyard lifting his big feet so high and stretching his head in the air:

"Cock-a-doodle-do!"

What a proud, handsome bird he is! And Mr Cock Chick has a lot to make him proud. Not only has he got the loudest voice:

"Cock-a-doodle-do!"

he has a pretty brown wife (as freckled and speckled as one of her eggs) and a fine family of five fluffy chicks. He also has a wonderful tail of curling, coiling, fiery feathers, green and orange and brown.

A fine family of five

The oldest and boldest of the baby Chicks is called Tiny. When he was young, how Tiny used to stare at that wonderful tail of his father's.

While his brothers and sisters ran about the farmyard, as soft and sunny as dandelions, Tiny Chick followed his daddy about, gazing at the wonderful tail.

He asked his mother, "Ma! Why haven't I got a lovely, big, curling, coiling, fiery tail? I want one! I want one! I do!"

Brown hen laughed cluckingly

The pretty brown hen put back her head and laughed cluckingly. "What would a little scrap like you do with a great tail like that? You're much too small to carry it!"

But Tiny Chick did not laugh. He ran along in the shadow of those fanned-out, furling feathers and he cheeped, "I want one! I want one! I want one! I do!"

Mr Cock Chick liked to be admired, and he crowed all the louder and showed off all the more, sitting on the roof of the barn for all the world to see.

Tiny Chick was so proud! But not every-body in the farmyard felt the same as he did. When Patrick Piggy came into the yard, Tiny said, "I bet you've come to see my Daddy's tail!"

"Uh? What? Who? Why?" grunted Patrick Piggy. "I haven't come to look at tails, I've come to look for acorns. What good are a few feathers? You can't eat them, can you?"

Tiny Chick was very angry. "You're only jealous because your tail is so small and ordinary. Ha! It looks like a wriggly worm!"

"You can talk! You can talk!" said Patrick Piggy. "You've got no tail at all!" And away he snuffled, his head down and his eyes on the ground. He never once looked up at the barn roof to admire Mr Cock Chick's wonderful tail, or listen to his wonderful crowing.

"Feathers? You can't eat them"

"He's only jealous because pigs don't grow feathers," thought Tiny Chick unkindly. "Imagine a pig with feathers! Ha ha ha!"

When Henry Hedgehog came by, Tiny Chick said, "I suppose you've come to see my Daddy's wonderful tail."

"How's that? Herrumph," said Henry. "I've come to look for spilled milk, not fancy feathers. What use are feathers? They don't frighten enemies away like my spines."

"You – you – *pin-cushion*! Just because you have no tail worth a mention!" said Tiny Chick rudely.

"Well neither have you!" said Henry, and he was so offended that he curled up in a ball.

"He's only jealous because hedgehog's don't grow feathers," thought Tiny Chick. "Imagine a hedgehog with feathers! Ha ha!"

When Barney Brown the rabbit hopped by, Tiny Chick said, "I expect you've come to see my Daddy's wonderful tail, since *you've* only got that puny powder-puff behind."

"If you want to get yourself a tail . . . make a proper job of it"

Foolish Tiny Chick! He should never have been rude to somebody as clever as Barney Brown.

"Oho! Is that what you think, you saucy chick?" said Barney, flicking his fluffy flash of a tail. "That's fine talk coming from *you*, my little tailless friend."

"Well one day I mean to have a tail like my Daddy's!" peeped Tiny Chick. "He has the best tail in the whole wide world!"

Barney Brown yawned. "Call that a tail? That's *nothing*. A peacock would make your Daddy look like a feather duster."

"What's a peacock?" asked Tiny Chick, too astonished to be upset.

"A peacock has a tail like the sea on a sunshiny day. He can fan the air into a gale with his thousand blue and purple feathers. If you want to get yourself a tail, don't get a puny one like your *Daddy's*. Get a peacock's tail!"

Tiny Chick was silent for a moment. Then he asked, in a shy little voice, "Could I?"

The first bird he met was **Mr Magpie**

Chapter Two

FINDING FEATHERS

"Could I?"

"Could you what, my little tailless one?"

"Could I get myself a tail?"

"Oh I dare say." There was a naughty gleam in Barney's eye. "If you collected a hundred feathers and tied them on where a tail should go, you might grow into a peacock – in time."

Tiny Chick leaped with joy. "Of course! . . . Oh but where can I get feathers?"

"From the birds, of course. Ask each bird in Brambledown Wood to give you a feather. Tell them you want to grow into a peacock. I'm sure they'll help. Now I must hop along. And away he went, ears shaking with laughter. Tiny did not stop to wonder why.

The first bird he met was the Magpie, as black and white as the keys of a piano.

Mr Magpie wagged his long black tail and shrieked with laughter when he heard how Tiny Chick wanted to grow into a peacock. But he gave a feather, even so.

Throstle Thrush laughed too

So did Throstle Thrush. His laugh was more sweet and musical than Mr Magpie's.

"Who put such an idea in your head?" he asked. So Tiny explained, and Mr Thrush nodded wisely. "I see Barney Brown means to teach you a lesson."

"What lesson's that?" asked Tiny Chick.

"Why, how to grow into a peacock, of course," said Throstle Thrush with a twinkle in his eye. "Here. I'll help you tie on this feather, and let's see what happens when you have visited all the birds." He was very clever with his beak, and he plucked a blade of grass and used it to tie his brown feather beside Mr Magpie's long, black quill.

"I already feel different and I only have two feathers. Maybe I should go and tell Ma about becoming a peacock. Won't she be proud!"

"Oh no! Don't do that!" squeaked a little voice close by. "Keep it for a surprise." Tiny looked round and saw Fanny Fieldmouse rolling on her back in fits of giggles. (She was a friend of Barney Brown and she knew what he was up to.)

"You're right," said Tiny Chick. "I'll wait till my peacock tail has grown. Imagine their faces *then*!"

"Imagine!" squeaked Fanny, holding her sides and kicking her feet in the air. "Te-he-he-he-he!"

Tiny was starting to feel as grand as any peacock: "I would like to talk with you, but I have work to do," he declared.

When Tiny had gone, Fanny ran through the wood spreading the news.

Fanny
Fieldmouse
spreading
the news

There are so many birds in Brambledown Wood. Tiny Chick walked a long, long way looking for each and every one.

"Mr Blackbird ... so glossy and black!"

"Oh Mr Blackbird! You are so glossy and black! Won't you spare me a feather for my tail?"

"Oh Mr Jay! Your suit is as bright as a paintbox! Won't you spare one feather to help me grow into a peacock?"

"Oh Rob Robin! What a rich, red waistcoat you have! Can you spare me a bright feather to help my tail grow?"

"Oh Mrs Finch! You're almost as yellow as I am! A feather of yours would suit me very well."

When the birds heard how Tiny wanted to grow into a peacock – and whose idea it was – they all gave a feather willingly. But as Tiny staggered away, carrying his collection of stiff feathers, he could hear Mr Jay or Mr Robin or Mrs Finch laughing fit to burst.

As Tiny Chick hopped happily along, he had a sudden thought.

"I wonder if a peacock can crow? Daddy can crow so loud he shakes the chimneypots and wakes up the cows in the morning. If a peacock's tail is even more wonderful than Daddy's tail, maybe a peacock can crow even louder and longer than a cockerel!"

And he stretched his little yellow neck and reached out his little yellow head and opened his little orange beak and *CROWED* for all he was worth.

"*Peep-cheep!*"

It wasn't exactly a cock-a-doodle-do. And it didn't sound much like a peacock. But it was loud enough to wake up *somebody* sleeping nearby.

"Goop-galloop! Good heavens! And *who*, may I ask, are *you*?"

Tiny Chick was so astonished by this deep voice that he dropped all the feathers he was carrying.

"Would you help me tie on these feathers?"

Chapter Three

THE WONDERFUL PEACOCK

"Oh Mr Toad! You startled me so much I dropped all my feathers!" cried Tiny Chick, gathering them all up again.

"Toad? *Toad?*" said the creature sitting on a stone in the pond. "I'm a frog-og. I'm Oggie the Frog-og."

"Oh, I'm so sorry, Mr Oggie, but I've never met a toad before."

"Frog-og! Frog-og! Frog-og!" bellowed Oggie leaping up and down on the spot. "I know what *I* am, but what in thunder are *you?*"

"Well just now I'm a chick, but soon I'll grow into a peacock." And Tiny Chick explained all about Barney and the feathers and the tail. ". . . So please would you help me tie on these feathers? It's very hard to reach."

"Oho-hoo-gloo-gloop!" gurgled the Frog, and laughed so hard that he fell off the stone and quite disappeared under water.

Tiny Chick stood and waited to see if Oggie would reappear. And while he waited he heard a voice high above his head, calling him:

"Hey! Hoi! You must be the Wonderful Peacock!" An acorn blipped him on the head. When Tiny Chick looked up, he saw Sam Squirrel's saucy face look-

"You must be the Wonderful Peacock"

ing out from a hole in a tree. "Good Morning, Most Wonderful Peacock, and how are you?"

"Me? Are you talking to me?" asked Tiny Chick. Then he danced a chicken-dance of joy. "It must be working! I must already be changing into a peacock! How thrilling! I do wish I could see myself!"

Barney Brown...
telling everybody

Of course he didn't know that Barney Brown had gone bounding from end to end of Brambledown Wood telling everybody about Tiny Chick's tail. And Fanny Fieldmouse had spread the gossip, too. Now every animal in tree, burrow or bush wanted to see the chick who thought he could grow into a peacock. Sam thought it was the funniest sight he had ever seen: "Isn't your tail very *heavy*, Most Wonderful Peacock?"

"It is a bit awkward," admitted Tiny, "but I'm sure it will get easier as I grow into a peacock." Sam laughed so much that he fell out of his tree.

He did not hurt himself because the ground beside the pool was soft with feathers left behind by the ducks. When Tiny Chick saw them, he gathered them up as fast as he was able. "More feathers for my beautiful peacock tail!"

Just then, Oggie the Frog swam back up from the bottom of the pool. He brought along Mrs Frog and their brood of children, and all their friends and relations, too. They all wanted to see the 'Wonderful Peacock.'

All over the pond, the fish were giggling: strings of silver bubbles rose up through the water. They leaped out of the waves to get a better view. "Come and see! Come and see the Wonderful Peacock! Ha-ha-hee!"

"Come and see! Come and see!"

"I must have changed lots and lots," thought Tiny. "Everybody in the world thinks I'm a peacock now!"

Oggie's children, the tadpoles, laughed until they spun round on their tails like tops: "When we are grown up, we shall *lose* our tails, not go looking for them!"

The tadpoles spun on their tails

"You're only jealous," said Tiny Chick, "because toads don't grow feathers."

"We won't be toads! We won't be toads! We'll be frog-ogs! Frog-ogs! Frog-og-ogs!" cried the furious little tadpoles, and they splashed him with water and made him drop all his feathers again.

But Oggie the Frog chased them away and, with his clever green fingers, he helped to tie Tiny's newest feathers in the place where a tail should go. He used strands of silkweed from the pond: oh how cold that was! But silk was the best weed for a peacock's tail.

Of course, while Oggie was at work, Tiny could not see the smile on his froggy face.

It was the same wherever he went in the wood. The birds called out, "Hey! Hoi! You must be the Wonderful Peacock!"

Mrs Crow swooped down to look him over with her beady

Mrs Crow swooped down

black eye, then gave him a long black feather off her back. Mr Pheasant rushed out from under a bush: "I must see . . . I must see . . . I must see the Wonderful Peacock!" But he gave a long, curling green feather – the best so far.

Mr Pheasant gave the best so far

So what if they did all whistle or hoot or chirrup or cackle with laughter as he went on his way? Tiny Chick didn't understand, so he didn't mind one bit.

In fact he promised to come back and show them when he was a peacock.

It was hard to balance with so many feathers tied where a tail should go. He was stumbling along a woodland path feeling very tired and unsteady, when he heard the beat of wings over his head.

"Aha! Some soft feathers for my nest!" thought Old Wise-Owl, and down he swooped. Tiny Chick felt two big claws grab him by the tail and – lo and behold! – he was flying through the air!

"Oh put me down, *please*!" he squealed.

Mr Wise-Owl was so astonished to find a voice attached to the feathers that he dropped Tiny at once and flew away. Tiny Chick landed softly – plop – on his tail. Inside his little yellow chest, his little heart was pattering like raindrops.

To cheer himself up, he gazed over his shoulder as he walked, admiring his great collection of feathers. He gazed and he gazed . . . so of course he could not see where he was going: *BIFF*!

"Oh do look where you're going!"

Chapter Four

TUMBLEDOWN CHICK

"Oh do look where you're going!" protested Maurice Mole. He lay flat on his back, where Tiny Chick had knocked him down, and he *stared*. "Marmalade and muffins! What in the world are you?"

"Can't you tell?" said Tiny, helping Maurice to his feet. "I am a peacock – at least I will be as soon as my tail has grown. It shouldn't take much longer."

"Well! If you're a peacock, I'm a tiger," said Mr Mole.

"I'm very pleased to meet you, Mr Tiger," said Tiny politely. "I would ask you for a feather, but I see tigers don't grow them. I shall come back and visit you when my tail has grown . . . and when I've learned how to keep my balance . . . *whoops*!"

Just then, a puff of wind picked up Tiny Chick by the tail and whirled and swirled him head-over-heels down the path. No sooner did he get to his feet than another gust of wind bowled and rolled him over and over – out of the woods, across a field, over a hedge and – bump! – right into Barney Brown the rabbit.

Barney was so pleased to see him that he grinned from one long ear to the other. "Ah, I see you are practising how to be a peacock! All peacocks have trouble with the wind while their tails are growing. And what a fine tail you've found for yourself, my clever little friend!"

Tiny got up, but the wind knocked him down again . . . and again and again. Over and over again. "Oh Mr Brown! It's awfully hard work being a peacock!"

"Nonsense! Just wait till you get home and show off to everyone in the farmyard."

"Yes, yes," agreed Tiny, "but how shall I ever get home like this?"

"It's awfully hard work being a peacock!"

"I shall help you, of course, my fine-feathered friend," said Barney.

"Oh thank you, Mr Brown! Ma will be worried about me, and it seems such a very long time since breakfast."

So Barney Brown led the way towards Brambledown Farm. And every time the wind blew down Tiny Chick, Barney picked him up again and dusted off his yellow fluff and straightened all his borrowed feathers.

High up in the trees, Mr Woodpecker hammered out the news with his beak for everyone to hear: *The Wonderful Peacock is going home! Make way for the Wonderful Peacock!*

Mole peered through his glasses

On the way, they passed many of the animals and birds Tiny had met on his search for feathers. Maurice the Mole peered through his thick glasses and shook his head. "If that's a peacock, I'm a kangaroo."

They passed Mr Magpie and Mrs Jay, Rob Robin, Mrs Finch and Throstle Thrush, Mr Blackbird and Mrs Crow. When they passed the woodland pond, Oggie the Frog and the tadpoles were still tittering, Sam Squirrel was still sniggering, and Fanny Fieldmouse was still lying on her back with her feet in the air, laughing fit to burst.

Mr Wise-Owl flew over Brambledown Wood and looked down at the fluffy yellow scrap with the great big bunching tail, and he shook his wise old head. "There goes one little chick that will have learned a lesson by bedtime tonight."

Tiny Chick was so tired. Oh the relief when the farmyard came into sight. He could see his father, Cock Chick, standing up on the roof of the barn, looking this way and that:

"Cock-a-doodle-do!
Tiny where are you?"

As they got closer, Tiny could hear the animals' oink-cluck-quack-moo-bleat-squeak.

"Time I was going," said Barney Brown the rabbit. (He did not want to meet up with Mr Cock Chick because he knew that cockerels can be very fierce indeed when they are angry.) So he straightened Tiny's wonderful tail one last time and sent him on alone, the last few steps of the way, through the open farmyard gate.

Every tree, every bush, every ditch and every hollow seemed to be full of giggles and whispers and a little pair of eyes looking out to see what would happen next.

Tiny Chick could see his brothers and sisters running around the yard, as soft and sunny as dandelions. He could see his mother, as speckled and freckled as one of her eggs. He ran forward as fast as he could go:

"Oh Ma! Ma! Look at me! I've got a tail and I'm going to grow into a peacock!"

Of course he tripped and tumbled in through the gate – a bundle of dust and feathers and fluff.

All the animals took a good look

Tiny Chick blew past Henry Hedgehog.

"What's that there?" said Henry as Tiny went rolling by. "Is it a tuft of straw out of the stables?"

Tiny Chick blew past Patrick Piggy.

"What's that there?" said Patrick as Tiny bowled by beneath his nose. "Is it a bird's nest blown out of a tree?"

"No, no! It's me! It's Tiny Chick! . . . I mean Tiny Peacock . . . I mean – I don't know what I mean. Oh Ma, *it's me*!"

Then all the animals in the farmyard gathered round to stare. Nobody stared harder than Mr and Mrs Chick, who couldn't believe their eyes.

"Oh Ma! I've come home!" cried Tiny. "What's the matter? Don't you recognize me? That's just because I'm growing into a peacock. Underneath my wonderful tail it's the same little me!"

"Oh Ma! It's me!"

So then Tiny Chick told the tale of his wonderful tail, although he was really too tired to speak, and his beak was so full of dust that talking was hard.

"I did so want a wonderful tail. So I asked all the birds in Brambledown Wood to give me one of their feathers. Barney Brown said that if I tied them where a tail should go, I would grow into a peacock. But oh dear, Ma, it is very hard to be a peacock until you get the hang of it. The wind blew me down and an owl picked me up and Henry Hedgehog thought I was a tuft of straw and Patrick Piggy thought I was a bird's nest . . . But I'm not! I'm not! I'm Tiny Chick!"

The pretty brown hen cocked her pretty brown head on one side and looked at him long and hard. At last she said: "Well, I don't know who you really are, but you're certainly not my Tiny Chick. You don't look anything like him," and away she went, high stepping on her pretty brown feet.

Everybody in the farmyard began to laugh

Chapter Five

WHO ARE YOU?

The doves in the dovecot began to coo: "Who are you? Who are you?"

Then suddenly everybody in the farmyard began to laugh.

The ducks quacked: "This is the famous Peacock."

The cows began to moo: "Do look at the foolish Peacock!"

The donkey began to bray: "See the funny-looking Peacock!"

The geese began to honk: "What a noodle-headed Peacock!"

Tiny's brothers and sisters, the other little Chicks began to peep, "Absurd!" "Ridiculous!" "Feather-brained Peacock!"

But Mr Cock Chick the cockerel held up one wing: "Enough! Cock-a-doodle-don't!

"If this young creature is foolish and vain, I suppose it's because his Daddy taught him to be. Watch out, or I might think you were laughing at Daddies, and then I would get very angry." (Of course after that nobody *dared* to laugh.) "Now, where's that rabbit Barney Brown? Wait till I get my claws on him! I'll teach him not to play practical jokes when I catch up with him!"

But although he flew up on to the roof of the barn and looked out to the north over Brambledown Wood, out to the east along the road, out to the west across the orchards and out to the south across the river, he did not spot Barney Brown loping away as fast as he could go. Just as well for Barney! It would probably be the last joke he played – for a while . . .

Barney Brown loping away

The evening wind blew. It caught in the feathers of Tiny Chick's wonderful tail and tumbled him round the farmyard. He might have blown clean away if Daddy Cock Chick had not flown down and stopped him with one big claw.

"Tell me now, Mr Wonderful Peacock," he said, "now you have met all the birds in Brambledown Wood and been a peacock for a day, which would you most like to be?"

Tiny Chick stood sadly with his feet crossed and his eyes on the ground. "Really and truly, I do wish I were Tiny Chick again . . . even though I did, I did, I did so want a wonderful tail."

Then everybody felt sorry for the dusty little chick. With his orange beak, Mr Cock Chick unpicked the blades of grass and strands of silkweed tying the mix of feathers where a tail should go.

The wonderful tail fell to the ground without a sound.

The wind picked it up and blew it away – clear over the roofs of the barn, the stables and the farmhouse.

"Goodness gracious! If it isn't my own son Tiny Chick!" exclaimed Cock Chick, pretending to be surprised.

Away ran Tiny Chick to find his mother behind the barn door. "Ma! Ma! Look, it's me!"

"Goodness gracious! If it isn't my own son, Tiny Chick!" she clucked, pretending to be astonished.

Then she spread wide her wings – as  speckled and freckled as one of her eggs – and she hugged Tiny Chick close to her soft brown breast-feathers.

"Oh Ma! Oh Ma! I know I'm silly, but I did, I did, I did so want a fine big tail like Daddy's!"

The wind blew it away

"And so you shall, you foolish little chick! Don't you realize? When you grow up, you'll have a tail just like Daddy's!"

"Hey! Hoi! Where's that peacock?"

Tiny was amazed. "But how, Ma! How? Must I go out and hunt for it? Or must I win a competition? Or must I buy it?"

"No, no, son. It will just grow. You don't have to do *anything* – except wait and be patient. Do you think you can do that?"

"Oh yes, oh yes!" cried Tiny Chick. "I'll be as patient as can be – so long as it grows soon. I do, I do, I do so want it to grow soon!"

Sometimes birds from Brambledown Wood flew over the yard and saw Tiny pecking for worms or chasing butterflies. "Hey! Hoi! Where's that Wonderful Peacock?" they called. "He said he'd come and show us his grown-up tail! Ha-ha-ha!" But Tiny took no notice at all.

Mr Wise-Owl saw...

As for the wonderful tail, Mr Wise-Owl found that and used it to line his nest. Next Spring he came flying to and fro over the yard looking for food to feed his young family. He saw Patrick Piggy rooting about for acorns. He saw Henry Hedgehog lapping up spilled milk. And of course he saw little yellow chicks pecking for worms and chasing butterflies, just like they always do in the Spring.

But none of them were Tiny Chick.

Tiny was sitting on the roof of the barn, beside his Daddy. On his head he wore a coxcomb as red as holly-berries. And spread out behind him – as lovely as a sunset – was a great big tail of curling, coiling, fiery feather in green and orange and brown. It was a big, bright, beautiful tail. Anybody could see that. And Tiny looked so *proud*.

Maybe you think he tied it on? He did not.

Maybe you think he borrowed his Daddy's? He did not.

As Tiny grew, so did his tail, and a more glorious tail you never saw in all your life.

Maybe you think he shows off a little bit, spreading his tail for all the world to see?

You're absolutely right.

But ask him, "Do you like your grown-up tail, Mr No-so-Tiny Chick?" and he will tell you:

"I do! I do! I cock-a-doodle-do!"

"I cock-a-doodle-do!"

The Bramb